The Frazzle Family Finds a Way

For my family—both the Frazzles and the Rosemarys among us
—Ann

G'mon now. . . . You know who you are.
—Stephen

The Frazzle Family Finds a Way

story by Ann Bonwill

pictures by Stephen Gammell

Holiday House / New York

The Frazzles were forgetful.

They forgot their umbrellas
when it rained.

They forgot their coats when it snowed and their sunscreen when it was sunny.

When they went off to work, Mrs. Frazzle forgot to comb her hair and Mr. Frazzle forgot to put on his trousers.

When they went off to school, Annie and Ben forgot that they weren't on vacation anymore.

Even Wags forgot where he'd buried his bone,
and none of the Frazzles could find it.

At the grocery store, the Frazzles forgot their list. "What do we need?" asked Mrs. Frazzle. But no one could remember. And so they forgot the milk and the bread and the apples, but they did get plenty of eggs.

Today's
Specials:
milk
bread
apples

They forgot where they'd parked the car. They forgot how to get home, and worst of all, they forgot Grandpa in the frozen food section.

That night they had a family meeting.
"Something must be done," said Mr. Frazzle.

And so Aunt Rosemary
came to stay.

Aunt Rosemary had ideas. "What you need is my system," she said. "It's guaranteed to work." She set about making notes and calendars and schedules and lists until it seemed that the whole house was covered in paper.

But the Frazzles were so forgetful that they forgot to bring their lists. And they forgot to look at their notes and consult their calendars and check their schedules too.

"Tsk," said Aunt Rosemary. "You are worse than I thought."

She made the Frazzles tie strings around their fingers to help them remember what they forgot. "My strings are foolproof," said Aunt Rosemary. "Surely they will work."

But
they
didn't.

"Tut," said Aunt Rosemary. "It seems you are hopeless." And she swooped off to the bathroom to soak in the tub.

Soon Annie heard something coming from the
bathroom. Aunt Rosemary's singing voice sounded
like Wags when the string around his tail was tied
too tightly, but it gave Annie an idea.

That afternoon at the grocery store . . .

. . . Annie sang a song!

Apples, lettuce, bread, and beets,
Chicken, carrots, chocolate treats,
Milk and cheese and one thing more,
Don't leave Grandpa at the store!

DEREK ANDERSON GROCERY STORE

Store
Closing
SALE

When they returned home,
Aunt Rosemary met them
at the door. "Tsk-tsk," she
said. "You forgot to bring
your list. And you left your
strings hanging from the
ceiling fan. I suppose it
will be twelve-egg omelets
for dinner again, with
egg sauce on the side."

"Nope!" said Ben. "We forgot our list, but we remembered everything on it."

And they had.

The next day the Frazzles sang another song.

~~Brush my teeth and come n~~

Brush my teeth and comb my hair,
Trousers are a must to wear.
Homework, schoolbag, and lunch box,
Trade my flippers for gym socks!

The day went much more smoothly, and all the Frazzles were happy. Even Aunt Rosemary. Because as it turned out, the Frazzles remembered something.

"My birthday!" said Aunt Rosemary. "I forgot!"

Text copyright © 2013 by Ann Bonwill
Illustrations copyright © 2013 by Stephen Gammell
All Rights Reserved
HOLIDAY HOUSE is registered in the U.S. Patent and Trademark Office.
Printed and Bound in October 2012 at Toppan Leefung, DongGuan City, China.
The text typeface is Pink Martini.
The artwork was created with colored pencil, watercolor paint, and pastel.
www.holidayhouse.com
First Edition
1 3 5 7 9 10 8 6 4 2

Library of Congress Cataloging-in-Publication Data
Bonwill, Ann.
The Frazzle family finds a way / by Ann Bonwill ; illustrated by Stephen Gammell. – 1st ed.
p. cm.
Summary: The Frazzle family is very forgetful, even when Aunt Rosemary visits and tries to straighten them out
with her system, until Annie finds a simple and effective way to remember.
ISBN 978-0-8234-2405-4 (hardcover)
[1. Memory–Fiction. 2. Family life–Fiction. 3. Humorous stories.] I. Gammell, Stephen, ill. II. Title.
PZ7.B6446Fr 2013
[E]–dc23
2011041929